SNAZZY CAT CAPERS

THE FAST AND THE FURRIEST

SNAZZY
CAT CAPERS

THE FAST AND THE FURRIEST

DEANNA KENT   ILLUSTRATED BY NEIL HOOSON

[Imprint]
MAKE YOUR MARK
NEW YORK

[Imprint]
MAKE YOUR MARK

A part of Macmillan Publishing Group, LLC
120 Broadway, New York, NY 10271

SNAZZY CAT CAPERS: THE FAST AND THE FURRIEST. Copyright © 2019 by GrumpyFish Creative, Inc. All rights reserved. Printed in the United States of America by LSC Communications, Harrisonburg, Virginia.

Library of Congress Control Number: 2018944990

ISBN 978-1-250-14347-1 (hardcover) / ISBN 978-1-250-14346-4 (ebook)

Our books may be purchased in bulk for promotional, educational, or business use. Please contact your local bookseller or the Macmillan Corporate and Premium Sales Department at (800) 221-7945 ext. 5442 or by email at MacmillanSpecialMarkets@macmillan.com.

Book design by Eileen Savage

Illustrations by Neil Hooson

Imprint logo designed by Amanda Spielman

First edition, 2019

1 3 5 7 9 10 8 6 4 2

mackids.com

FFBI Official Bulletin:
Attention, cat burglars: Book thievery is not deemed honorable by the
Furry Feline Burglary Institute. Those who do not comply will be cursed
with twitchy whiskers and inventors who can't stop with the knock-knock jokes.

For Sam, Max, Zach, Jake, Jackson, Ethan, Ella, Anna, Colton,
and everyone who chases the chaos of creativity,
a ball of yarn, or (gasp) balls and bones.

FUR-WORD

She's an international kitty of mystery—a classy cat burglar with more dapper disguises and purr-fect plans than I have inventions. Wherever you go, watch for Ophelia von Hairball V of Burglaria, the master of heists and hijinks. As reported by *The Meow Zine* (TMZ) and *Enter-tail-ment Weekly,* this cat manages to "follow the time-honored cat burglar code without paws-ing for a beat." If **you** spot this snazzy cat on an exciting adventure, please let me know right away . . . **because I was supposed to go with her!**

—*Oscar F. Gold (Inventor #17)*

"Be the fabulous you want to see in the world."

—Ophelia von Hairball V

1

NEED FUR SPEED

It was hot enough to fry catnip on the sidewalk, but nobody paid attention to the snazzy feline sauntering down the Las Vegas strip in her massive motorcycle helmet and protective leather outfit.

"Hey, fancy pants! Watch it!"

Daydreaming, the disguised Ophelia wasn't

paying attention to where her fur-tastic tail was flicking, to and fro.

"WHOAA!" One particularly sassy tail flick knocked over a cart packed to the brim with glitter-bombs. As the sparkly packages smashed onto the road, a multicolored explosion made the street shine and shimmer.

"Oops!" Ophelia stopped to fix the disaster her overenthusiastic tail had caused. "So sorry." She helped the owner stand the cart back up. Surveying the sparkle, she handed over some money to pay for the merchandise. Ophelia smiled. "May I just say . . . this street looks much more fabulous—as does everything—covered in glitter!"

With the kind of flair she normally saved for masquerade balls and wingsuit landings, the infamous Ophelia and her floofy tail continued past a giant pirate ship, a gurgling fountain, massive lion statues (which elicited an involuntary meow from Ophelia), and even a replica of the Empire State Building. Finally, she arrived at her hotel: a great big pyramid. It was a grand spectacle! *Just like me.* She smiled to herself, then checked her watch and felt a whisker-twitching thrill. It was almost time! In just moments, she'd have—

Buzz. Garble. "Ophebrrrzxxxx. OPHELRIXR-ASCOBZ!"

As Ophelia entered the hotel lobby, a series of high-pitched screeches through the motorcycle helmet receiver made her jump. She couldn't take the helmet off—it was a purr-fect disguise! Ophelia felt around for an off switch but instead found only a mysterious gold button on the outside strap. Ophelia knew better than to push it.

"OPHELIA!" The shrill, aquatic voice on the other end grew a little bit clearer. But it didn't sound particularly happy, so Ophelia tried to ignore it. Right now she had zero time for a fish inventor who was (more than likely) mad at her.

Her silent treatment didn't stop the fish from nattering in her ear. "Ophelia von Hairball V! Hello? Are you there? Helloooo? Wow. Um. Are you ignoring me?" Oscar asked. Ophelia imagined his little fins flapping with frantic frustration. "Seriously, Ophelia, if you can hear me, I've been trying to find you for *days*. Your signal showed up in Chicago, Istanbul, Kelowna, and Tokyo. Did you—?"

"Yes." Ophelia interrupted him. "Yes, yes, *yes*," she confessed. (Sometimes it's easier to just confess.) "There was a row of identical motorcycle helmets on the highest shelf in your lab. I nabbed them, turned on their beacons, boxed up each one, and mailed them to different cities around the globe."

Oscar sounded stunned. "Why in the name of Poseidon would you do *that*?"

"To be really honest, it was a rather desperate attempt to have some alone time. But you found me. I was fairly confident I'd turned off the beacon in *this one*, though."

"Hrumph. Yes, but I include backups in most of my designs," Oscar told her.

A note of admiration crept into Ophelia's voice. "You're rather sneaky, aren't you?"

Oscar Fishgerald Gold was Ophelia's seventeenth inventor. She'd worked very hard to ditch all of her previous sidekicks, as she preferred to burgle on her own. Before Oscar showed up on the doorstep of her lair, she had rejected sixteen inventors for a variety of *very* valid reasons.

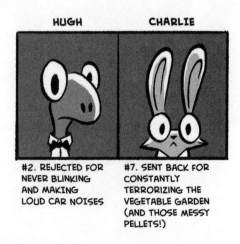

HUGH CHARLIE

#2. REJECTED FOR NEVER BLINKING AND MAKING LOUD CAR NOISES

#7. SENT BACK FOR CONSTANTLY TERRORIZING THE VEGETABLE GARDEN (AND THOSE MESSY PELLETS!)

ADDISON

NORMAN

#10. FOR CHEATING AT MEW-NOPOLY AND DISLIKE OF BLACK LICORICE

#16. FOR HIS TERRIBLE SINGING, OUT-OF-CONTROL BUG PHOBIA, AND THOSE ENDLESS KNOCK-KNOCK JOKES

Known for her legendary capers, Ophelia von Hairball V was the Furry Feline Burglary Institute's number-one cat burglar. *Other* burglars seemed to need (and even want) inventors, but Ophelia took special pride in upholding the classy, time-honored traditions of the FFBI *alone*. Until Oscar, she'd managed to stay 100 percent inventor-less. She'd tried to return him when he'd first arrived, too. But MEW, director of the FFBI, had insisted that she keep him. To be fair, Oscar had proven himself quite useful with his superior gear, gadgets, and fashion designs. But Ophelia still liked to work solo.

Most FFBI cat burglars (especially the elite ones) treated each heist as an opportunity to hone their skills. They performed purr-fect crimes with a touch of elegance and a dash of dare. It was all about the thrill of the chase. And (though it sometimes took a bit longer to return very, very pretty things), they gave back what they pilfered.

The exception? The FFBI's *second-best* burglar, Pierre von Rascal of Thievesylvania, who was (regrettably) Ophelia's nefarious cousin and

archenemy. He was not classy in *any* way. Ever since they'd been kittens, he'd been jealous of Ophelia.

Oscar's voice crackled loudly. "You *can't* ignore me, Ophelia! I've disabled the mute button on all your built-in receivers."

Ophelia rolled her (lovely) eyes. "Please get out of my ear, fish-face. I'm on vacation—I *deserve* a holiday! Some shopping, some pampering"—she looked down at her claws—"and a manicure! I'm spoiling myself." She didn't mention that she'd been mixing a *teensy* bit of business with her fun.

"A vacation? What kind of FFBI cat burglar leaves for vacation without telling their paw-rtner in crime, their soulmate in crime capers?!"

"'Soulmate in crime capers'? Stop it. You're my inventor, Oscar," she reminded him.

"One minute I'm krilling myself to craft you a swanky disguise, and the next minute I'm alone. Are you *really* not going to steal a single thing in Las Vegas? You're just enjoying a heist-free holiday?"

"Well," Ophelia conceded, looking at all the

glitz and glamour surrounding her, "there are a *few* sparkly baubles here and there. I *could* be persuaded to come home with a souvenir."

"Sounds like I should be wherever you are," Oscar pouted.

"You know that glorious Mini-Ultra-Teeny-Tiny Sticker Cam you constructed last week?"

"The M.U.T.T.S.C.?! Sure. It has real potential! But it hasn't been tested yet."

"Well . . . I saw it in your lab, and it looked quite functional," Ophelia told him. "In fact, it looked so *fin*-tastic that I brought it with me. It's attached to the divine motorcycle helmet I'm wearing. You can test it now, if you'd like. Go on," Ophelia prodded him. "Start it up so you can see everything I see in real time. That's almost as good as being here!"

"Well, it's *something*," Oscar retorted. "But it's NOT almost as good as being there. And just so you know, I will be triple-locking my lab from now on. I think it's only fair that if you want to use my inventions, you must take me with you—I want in on the action!"

"Oh, Oscar," Ophelia sighed. "A triple-locked door? You're kitten me. Too easy. Anyhow, you'd hate the desert. Personally, I think the lack of water here is *divine*. But you'd be a puckered-up, dried-out prune fish in no time." She chuckled at the thought.

"You know better than anyone how well my S.P.I.T. works!" Oscar's Small Portable Inter-water Tank invention allowed him to be on dry land for long periods of time. "And last time, in Paris, you promised you'd take me on the next heist!"

She shook her head. "No. You *wanted* me to promise. But I did nothing of the sort."

OPHELIA! I COULD HAVE MADE YOU AN INCREDIBLE **ELVIS OUTFIT** FOR VEGAS. IT WOULD HAVE BEEN THE DREAMIEST DESIGN EVER.

I WON'T BE ABLE TO STOP THINKING ABOUT IT NOW!

FISH, LESS CONVERSATION AND **MORE ACTION.**

"Stop with the tantrum and turn on the helmet camera so you can see my genius at play," Ophelia suggested.

"Okay," Oscar sighed and connected the camera's signal to his lab's big screen. The fish could see everything through Ophelia's helmet camera. "Nice! The M.U.T.T.S.C. works well! You're live."

Ophelia swiveled her head so Oscar could get a panoramic view. She imagined Oscar back at home, his little fish-face squashed to the monitor, hoping to see every detail.

"Good picture. Ultra HD, 4K video quality. Um, Ophelia? Why are there a zillion balloons directly above your head? You detest balloons!"

While it was true that balloons usually made her fur stand on end, for this heist to work, Ophelia was depending on them.

"Wait a second. Are you in a pyramid?!" Oscar questioned.

"Why, yes. A purr-amid of sorts," she revealed. She heard the fish typing. He was an excellent researcher.

"Have you pinpointed my location yet?" she asked.

"Of course." The key-clicking got faster. "Nevada. The Luxor Hotel on the Las Vegas Strip?"

Ophelia grinned.

"I'm scanning the hotel's guest list now," he told her. "I bet I can guess what you're trying to steal! Horace B. Fuzzbuttsworth is checked in with his prized Rolex collection. . . . Or, wait! Queen Basta is there, too—with the incredible pearls she won at the Sotheby's auction last week. . . ."

"But you know I prefer old-fashioned timepieces. And I already have exquisite pearls. They're in my secret lair. Hmm. I should wear those pearls again soon. Would you mind dusting them while I'm out of town?"

"Dust? I think not! I'm a *senior* inventor! I have more IQ points than you have hats!" He sighed.

Ophelia moved her head around to give Oscar one more good look at the hotel lobby. "Anyway, I'm not here for the pearls. You're missing the

obvious, fish! Remember the challenges the FFBI issued after the last heist?"

"I've got them here," Oscar told her, confused.

"This mini Vegas vacay was a purr-fect excuse to check off another priceless treasure. I do need to stay ahead of the other burglars. Especially Pierre. That scoundrel—"

"*GASP!*" The gilled gadget guru sucked in his breath as he suddenly figured out the real reason Ophelia von Hairball V of Burglaria, cat burglar extraordinaire, was at the Luxor Hotel in Las Vegas, Nevada.

"Never say never. Unless you're talking about mushy peas. Or dogs."

—Ophelia von Hairball V

2

VIVA, DIVA

Through the M.U.T.T.S.C. stuck to Ophelia's helmet, Oscar could see that she was standing in front of ten of the world's most expensive motorcycles. Each bike was encased in a separate thick, glass case. There were several grumpy-looking guards in front of them.

"Ooooooh. The motorcycle show . . ." Oscar

exclaimed, awestruck. "Please turn toward the gold one, Ophelia."

She swiveled her (fabulous) head.

"It's outstanding!" Oscar couldn't take his bulgy eyes off the gold-plated chopper. "That one would match *me*." His voice was thick with daydreams. "You could drive. I'd build a smashing sidecar, and I'd paint our Oscar and Ophelia 'O²' logo on the side. And just think of the gold racing outfits I could make. . . ." His voice trailed off as he continued to scan the glass cases. "Oh, wait. Hold on to your hairballs! Is that a—"

"Yes," Ophelia interrupted. "It is the one and only Sooperbike. It's the fastest. It's the lightest." She smiled. "And it's *expensive*. Almost four million dollars, I'm told. But that's not the one I'm going to liberate and enjoy. Watch this, fish."

Ophelia took a tiny laser from her special-ops handbag. She turned it on and pointed the green beam above her. There was the *snap* of a net breaking. And, a moment later, from the pyramid's ceiling, hundreds and hundreds of balloons fell. The guards threw their suspicious gazes upward. The crowd oohed and aahed.

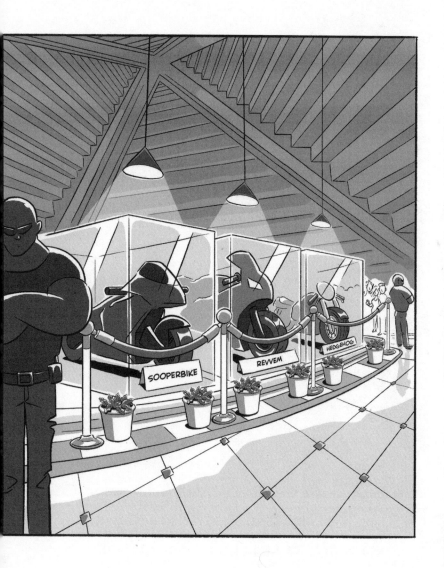

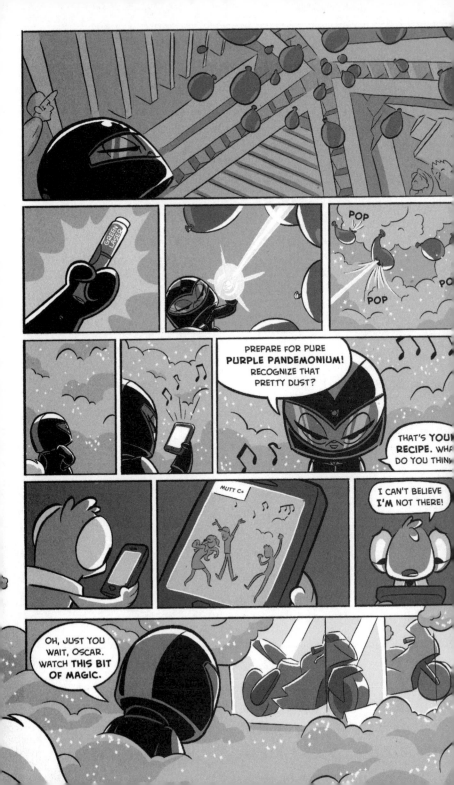

Once Ophelia was outside and hidden in the traffic of the crowded Las Vegas strip, Oscar's questions started again. "How on earth did you manage that?"

"Easy, my dear inventor. Just a few simple steps. Earlier today, I did some balloon shopping. Though I hate balloons, they are purr-fect for holding the pretty purple dust and sparkle I used as a distraction. And the speakers were simple to set up. Did you love the music? I turned it on and everyone assumed it was an impromptu party!"

"But the glass," Oscar prompted. "How did you make a *whole glass case* disappear?"

"Ah. Going through the glass was easy . . . because *there was no glass*. It was a hologram, though it looked exactly like the other glass cases."

"You mean there was no case around that bike all day?" Oscar asked. "It was an illusion?"

"That's right. No glass. Just a few inattentive guards."

"And the key to get the motorbike started?" Oscar pressed.

"Darling fish, you know I never let a little vault get in the way of anything."

Ophelia expertly maneuvered the motorbike in and out of traffic until she saw the semi-trailer truck she'd been looking for. It was driving down the highway at a steady speed. As she approached it, a ramp lowered from the back and she rode up into the truck.

Inside, she stepped aside while a few of her international FFBI allies did a very fast, very pink paint job to disguise the bike. Then she drove back out.

Suddenly, Oscar was in her ear again, his voice serious. "Code Flea! Ophelia, the FFBI just issued an alert. It's top priority. You need to get home. There's an emergency meeting first thing tomorrow morning. All members must attend via video conference."

"Code Flea? *Wow. Meow.* That's reserved for *very*

urgent things." Ophelia took a deep breath and hissed with disappointment. "I love the feeling of the wind in my fur. I had hoped to take a few days and slowly drive home. I've always wanted to see Roswell." Of course, Ophelia wouldn't dream of being late for a meeting with the FFBI. Besides being a dedicated cat burglar, being on time was one of her trademarks. "Would you please send the FFBI helicopter to pick me up just outside of Crystal Springs?"

"I can do better." Oscar sounded smug. "If you press the small gold button on the strap of your motorcycle helmet, you won't need a ride."

"I found that button already. I won't push it until you tell me *exactly* what it will do. And don't be vague."

The fish sighed. "One day you'll just trust me and not ask. But today, that particular gold button will give you a very speedy jet-boost."

"Is it safe?" She hesitated. "I don't want to mess up my manicure. Or, you know, the weather system, plant life in the area, or my internal organs."

"I'm offended," Oscar retorted, pretending

to be offended. But it was true that a recent gold button demonstration had seen Oscar twirl up a handcrafted tornado. It had been messy. "For your information, there are safety features embedded in that helmet that NASA would scratch for."

Ophelia grinned, took a deep breath, pushed the button, and away she went. If the cat had checked her rearview mirror, she might have noticed a mysterious figure wearing an old-fashioned fedora in a low-flying jet who followed her all the way home.

"I love neon jelly beans, long belly rubs, and when a purr-fect plan comes together."

—Ophelia von Hairball V

3

SUIT UP WITH STYLE

In her lair, sprawled out on a windowsill with her velvet sleep mask over her eyes, Ophelia was basking in the sun.

But as the relaxing minutes ticked by, the sun moved in the sky and her fur was suddenly not as warm. She decided to finally put the robotic dog, which her pesky goldfish inventor had built without her permission, to work.

Oscar came tearing over, his face pinched with panic. "P.U.G.! Cancel Ophelia's last command. Please gently pick Ophelia up and move her two inches to the right at 0.002 miles per hour, so she's in the center of the sun rays coming through the window." He shook his head. "Ophelia! How many times do I need to remind you? P.U.G. is coded to interpret everything very literally. Although I'm curious to see how it would figure out a way to get you to the middle of the sun, let's not do that today."

Oscar had handcrafted P.U.G. to resemble the nosy next-door neighbor dog to try to impress

Ophelia. It hadn't worked. "I'm really not a fan of that metal abomination," she said, stretching from paw to paw. "Seriously, if I have to make an extra effort to not be sent to the center of the sun, then I'd rather just do things mysel—"

She pulled her sleep mask off to finish her tirade against the robo-dog but stopped when she saw her fish inventor's new look.

"Ta-da!" Oscar posed for her. "What do you think? Do you like my new hair?" He fish-flexed. "I pity the feline who messes with this fish!"

Oscar the goldfish, usually quite conservative and plain, had on a thick Mohawk wig and a sleek, sleeveless camo lab coat. Ophelia's whiskers dropped. She was speechless. (That was rare.)

Oscar grinned. "I knew you'd be surprised! I love creating disguises, gadgets, and gear, but I rarely design for myself. What do you think? I saw someone like this on an old TV show and thought he looked super tough!"

"There was absolutely nothing wrong with your previous, not-so-tough look. However," she admitted, "'live and let live' is my motto. And this style is fairly fabulous on you."

"I'm not sure if it's going to be my permanent style," he told her. "I'm exploring."

"Feel free to borrow my wigs and costumes," Ophelia offered generously.

Almost as soon as the words escaped from her mouth, she wished she could suck them back in. "But not the ones in my vault," she clarified.

"Speaking of disguises . . ." Oscar presented Ophelia with a gift-wrapped box. "I'm not sure if you deserve this," he teased, "after you didn't take me to Las Vegas. But during our Himalayan diamond heist, I promised I'd make this for you."

Curious, Ophelia took the box. "*Pour moi?*" she asked, tearing open the paper right away. Inside was a sleek, black, shiny cat burglar suit. Ophelia had never seen anything so gorgeous. "*Purr.* Oscar! It's magnificent!"

"The design is quite unique." He beamed, thrilled that she loved it. "I might patent it. Try it on!"

Ophelia stepped into the suit and checked herself out in the mirror. "In this moment," she gushed, "I'm glad I didn't return you to the FFBI. Because *this* is amazing."

"Just wait until you see the top-notch gadgets I've integrated," Oscar declared. He'd spent the last month toiling over secret gear Ophelia

could use when she was in heist mode. "And the best part?" he continued. "I have a matching sui—" Unexpectedly, P.U.G. marched in front of them and blurted, "SOLDIERS! Prepare for an incoming FFBI call. Five point zero minutes. GO! GO! GO!" Surprised and frightened at the sudden loud noise, Ophelia jumped and landed claws-first on the silk curtains.

"What is happening?!" Ophelia forgot the warm and fuzzy paw-rtnership she'd felt for Oscar just moments before. She pounced back onto the floor and put her furry face right up against his portable tank unit. His S.P.I.T. was the only thing between the cat's fury and his wide eyes. "*Why* is that robo-dog *talking*?" she hissed. "It's bad enough when it's totally silent!"

"Don't worry, Ophelia. I'm just doing a little experiment. P.U.G. needs a voice! It's so hard to pick just one. So far, I've got about one hundred different voices. For instance, there's Scooby-Doo, Lumpy Space Princess—and that one you just heard was a generic *yelling coach* voice." Oscar felt the intensity of Ophelia's piercing glare. "But I'm sensing that you aren't loving it."

"No, I am not 'loving it.' No, no, *NO!*"

"Okay." He nodded. "You're not a fan of the coach. I get it. Please don't fret, because every time P.U.G. talks, we'll hear someone different! Plus there are sound effects. Some are dog-like. Some are—well, er, um … experimental." Ophelia hissed, but Oscar continued.

"And not to alarm you, but there's a smidgen of a glitch right now where P.U.G. sometimes bursts into random song. No worries! It's not like karaoke in the least. I've done a temporary fix on the singing issue and set an obscure code phrase. It's the only thing that will trigger a song. P.U.G. will only bust out a song if you say—"

Ophelia's eyes were huge, and her anger made her forget her manners. She interrupted. "*Voices? Singing?* All of this is *ludicrous!* Oscar, when you're not looking, I'm definitely unplugging the bot-mutt," Ophelia stated.

"How many times do I have to tell you that you can't unplug it, because it's NOT plugged in? P.U.G. runs on a very efficient solar-powered panel. And unless you shut down the sun, you will NOT shut down P.U.G."

The lights on the communication center went on then, and Ophelia took a deep breath. She tried not to think about P.U.G. and its new voices.

MEW would be calling at any moment with a brand-new challenge to take on. In anticipation, Ophelia did a good fur fluff.

"MEW's latest security requirements for the lair are over the top," Oscar mentioned to Ophelia as he punched a long code into the computer. Recently, upon orders from Director MEW, Oscar had upgraded all FFBI cat burglars' secret-lair security systems. There were new locks, high-resolution security cameras, and cutting-edge noise filters that ensured nobody could listen in on their conversations.

Oscar turned to his robot assistant. "P.U.G.! Quickly scan the latest security measures in the lair, please." He pinched his fish lips together and glanced sideways at Ophelia. "And I'd like a *verbal* report."

P.U.G. slowly pirouetted, surveying the new programs. Then its voice boomed like a sports announcer into a microphone. "Security measures are out of the park!"

Ophelia put her head in her paws, but before she could stage a hiss-y fit, her phone lit up, and she refocused. ***PURRRR. PURRRR.*** Code Flea! All the cats would soon be calling in to find out what was so urgent.

Ophelia adjusted some light reflectors around her seat, put a recently pilfered emerald tiara on her head, and placed the purr-fect Himalayan diamond in front of her. She made sure her number-one cat burglar trophy was extra shiny and reflected the dark sheen off her new cat burglar suit. *Tiara, gem, and trophy—a trifecta of claw-someness!*

"What do you think, Oscar?" Ophelia asked. "Will Pierre just love this or what?"

The screen in front of her lit up with the images of other FFBI agents joining the call. Oscar looked over to Ophelia and her props, and his eyes bulged. He whispered, "The emerald tiara? The Himalayan diamond? *And* the trophy?

Do you really want to show off like that? Won't Pierre want *ALL* the revenge?"

Muting her FFBI microphone, she replied, "There's no point having the talent to pilfer priceless objects if you can't fully enjoy them. This tiara needs to be worn one last time, because it will soon be on its way back to its rightful castle. Besides, I earned these trinkets fair and square. With style! With class! With panache—"

Oscar interrupted, "—*with my help.*"

Right on time, Director MEW's face filled half of Ophelia's monitor.

But in a corner of the screen, Ophelia noted Pierre's unibrow was in an angry perma-squint today. Behind Pierre, she caught a glimpse of Norman.

Norman was Ophelia's former inventor—number sixteen. She hadn't enjoyed his too-loud singing and never-ending knock-knock jokes, so once she'd discovered his fear of bugs (after only two days), it was easy to persuade him that they weren't a good match.

"Good morning, elite burglars." Director MEW's voice was scratchy, as if she hadn't slept.

"We have a lot to talk about and not much time."

Whatever was happening at FFBI HQ seemed to be a huge, hairy deal.

"Not everyone will adore what you do. That's purr-fectly fine. Do what makes you feel shiny."

—Ophelia von Hairball V

4

SASS & CLASS

Right away, MEW looked at Ophelia. "First, let's congratulate Ophelia von Hairball V on her latest victory. As you know, Ophelia's diamond escapade won her the FFBI's Fifth Annual Purr-fect Heist Competition, cementing her title as number-one cat burglar."

All eyes on her, Ophelia beamed into the camera and turned on a not-so-bashful smile. She shifted slightly to allow the lights around her to hit her tiara's emeralds and form beautiful green glimmer-bursts. "Ophelia, your ongoing commitment to classy and classic burglary techniques is an inspiration to our organization."

She hoped her cousin was paying close attention to the paw-clapping for her victory. During the Purr-fect Heist Competition, Pierre had stooped to new levels to try and win the Himalayan diamond. To secure the diamond and the title of number-one cat burglar, Ophelia had been forced to *swim* (her least favorite activity). Pierre had even fish-napped Oscar! It all just showed how Pierre was a disgrace to the FFBI and cat burglars everywhere. He was most unclassy!

MEW spoke, and Ophelia felt a small shiver of excitement that made her furr fluff. "Please get out your laptops and take notes." Ophelia preferred paper to electronics, and the director's seriousness warranted some old-fashioned opulence, so she took out her antique fountain pen and a bottle of ink.

"Cats, the FFBI is facing our most important challenge to date. More than a century ago, elite members of the FFBI discovered that there was a rival organization trying to destroy them. Today, you know that organization as the Central Canine Intelligence Agency. Right from the beginning, the CCIA wanted nothing more than to put a stop to our stealing stylings and bring *paw and order* to the world. As such, years ago they created a contraption that was very dangerous to cats." MEW looked at her team intently. "But just before they could start it up, a few very talented members of the FFBI got their claws on this invention."

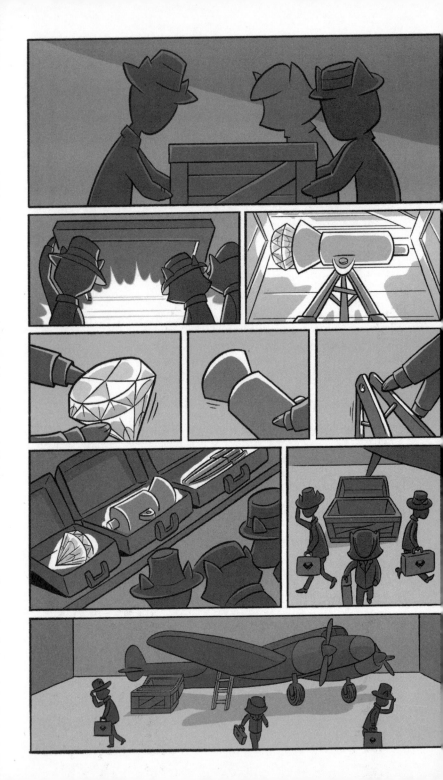

"You mean the FFBI stole the invention from the CCIA?" asked Pierre.

"Indeed—they stole it. They couldn't risk bringing it intact to the FFBI headquarters, so they split it into three pieces and hid those pieces around the globe. Then, they gave me the encrypted map to keep safe. When solved, it tells the location of the first piece of the device. I kept it safe. It was inside our underground, super-sonic, triple-locked vault."

Was? Ophelia's ears perked up.

MEW paused for a moment. Nobody dared to twitch a whisker. "If someone breaks the map's encryption, they can find the first piece of the device. Once they have the first device piece, they will discover the next encrypted map—which leads to the location of the second piece. And once they find the second piece, they get the last encrypted map and can find the final piece of the device."

On-screen, Pierre yawned rudely.

MEW continued, "For almost a century, the

first map has been secured here at FFBI HQ. Until yesterday, that is. Last night at midnight, our vault was compromised and the map was stolen." Several sets of cat eyes opened wide. "Thankfully, I'd made a copy."

All the cats were wondering the same thing, but inquisitive, elite cat burglar Penelope from Milan was the first to ask: "Just what *is* this device? Is it dangerous? What can it do?"

Director MEW didn't blink. "This information is highly classified. It is"—she leaned forward in her seat, and Ophelia could see MEW's concern—"a massive, powerful laser pointer code-named *Scarlet Claw*," MEW explained, her voice lowered. "This device is *so large*, *so red*, and *so bright* that if

it fell into the wrong hands, it would immediately captivate all cats. We would be under *complete control* of whomever was operating it. Since we stole it, we've talked of creating protective measures against the Scarlet Claw's powerful laser beam, but it was never a priority. Until now."

"Did the CCIA sneak into the FFBI HQ vault and take the encrypted map?" Ophelia inquired.

MEW grimaced. "We assume so but have no way to know. Our cameras were taken down. We're investigating."

Pierre spoke up. "So are we all going to look for this old thing or what? Let's all meet up and go after it before those dumb dogs find it!"

"Actually, after careful deliberation," MEW stated without emotion, "the FFBI has chosen our top cat burglar, Ophelia, for this difficult international mission. Some of you will be deployed to different global locations as decoys," she said, "but we believe that we have the best shot at finding the pieces quickly if Ophelia is focused on the case. Everyone needs to support her."

Pierre, bitter because he was always ranked

the *number-two* cat burglar, scrunched his face, making his unibrow look like a squashed caterpillar. "Pshh, not fair!" He stuck his tongue out at Ophelia.

On the screen, Ophelia could see Pierre's frustration as he clutched and squeezed a very familiar action figure. When they were young, Pierre had stolen Captain Claw-some from Ophelia, and it was her purr-sonal mission to one day get the toy back.

She cringed and quietly confessed to Oscar, "As much as I love these jewels, I'd trade them all to get Captain Claw-some back, you know."

"Don't kid yourself. Pierre's not trading with *you* for anything," Oscar whispered. "Well . . . maybe for the title of number-one cat burglar."

MEW ignored Pierre's childish outburst. "Make no mistake: Every single agent here is on red alert—*scarlet* alert! All of you—and that includes you, Pierre—will help Ophelia with *whatever* she needs, *wherever* she is. Ophelia, I can't believe I'm saying this, but you have an unlimited budget and unlimited resources."

Ophelia's tail swished excitedly. This was a *legendary* mission!

"And one more thing," MEW cautioned. "We have disturbing reports from New York, Montreal, and London that the Central Canine Intelligence Agency will be hot on our tails. As you know, they want to shut down the FFBI. We need to remain on high alert. Especially you, Ophelia. Always assume that you are being followed. Use whatever means necessary to disguise yourself, and stay ahead of everyone. Be fast!"

"I'm fabulous—the fastest and the furriest!" Ophelia chimed in just as her doorbell rang.

"Go get the door, Ophelia!" MEW commanded. "That's the copy of the first encrypted map. Use it to find the first piece of the device. Buried with the first piece of the device will be the next map. Please get to work immediately. We can't waste any time. Whomever was in our vault will be trying to break the map's code before you do."

Ophelia smiled and stood up. "Thank you,

Director MEW." She nodded to the whole feline team. "I'll do us all proud." With a pleased meow, she signed off the call and went to the door. An FFBI special-delivery cat handed Ophelia a black box.

"Merci beaucoup," she told her ally. Excitement churned like a windstorm in Ophelia's stomach. As she closed and locked her front door, she failed to notice the shadowy figure in her prizewinning rosebush who was watching her every move.

"To be fabulous or not to be fabulous? That is the question. Except it's a ridiculous question because we all know the answer."

—Ophelia von Hairball V

5

MAPS & MEW-SEUMS

Ophelia set the box on her table and stared at it for a few seconds. *This is the most epic caper of my career.* She looked around for her fin-ventor, who was nowhere to be found. "Oscar! Where are you? This is a very important moment for me. Don't you want to see me open this box?" She shed her suit and tiara, but she was too curious to wait any longer for him.

With a deep breath, one layer at a time, Ophelia carefully opened the box and unwrapped the first map from its padding.

Oscar emerged from his lab, wearing a different wig. Ophelia raised a (purr-fectly manicured) eyebrow. "Another new look?"

"Just trying a Nancy Mew style to see if it helps me solve the first code!" He scooted over and raised up his tank lab to get a closer look. "That's it?" His fin flapped over the map. "Director MEW didn't mention that this would be such a *cryptic* puzzle. There's literally nothing here to help us find the first piece of the Scarlet Claw!"

"That negativity isn't very Nancy Mew of you." Ophelia saw several things on the paper that she was excited about. "Take a closer look, fin-face."

Ophelia put on a pair of silk gloves. Then she reached into the black box and held the map up. "This paper tells a story. You just have to be willing to think outside the tank a bit, Oscar."

"Well," he pouted, sticking out his fish lips, "I wish you'd share, because it sounded like MEW is in a big hurry for us to find the first piece of the device! If I don't even know where we're going, how can I get us there? How can I make us the appropriate disguises and gadgets that will help us *save the world*?"

Ophelia gave Oscar (and his impressive fish pout) a dismissive paw-wave. "Are you trying to be cute? It's *me* who is going to save the world. Not *us*. Not *we*!" Ophelia ignored her inventor's extraordinary display of disappointment. "Here. Take a look." She held out the delicate paper for him to inspect. "See the thickness of this paper? It's papyrus. I've seen several examples in mewseums around the globe."

"Papyrus originated in ancient Egypt. That's our first clue." She smiled. "Our second is this triangle. Looks like a pyramid, right? *Oscar, I'm going to Egypt.*"

"Okay. But isn't Egypt a big place? Shouldn't you be aiming for a more specific location?"

"Yes, of course," Ophelia admitted, her whiskers twitching with the thrill of the challenge. "I'll definitely need to narrow it down."

"Wait a moment!" Oscar used his magnifying monocle. "What are these numbers underneath these symbols?"

"Maybe it's a secret code to crack?"

Oscar flipped his wig back dramatically. "What if that's simply the latitude and longitude?" He punched the numbers into his tablet and beamed at Ophelia. "It's the Mew-seum of Egyptian Antiquities—the Cairo Mew-seum in Egypt!"

Ophelia meowed with joy. "Excellent work, fish! I'm going to Cairo. Please unearth the blueprints for the mew-seum and be ready to go in an hour. I'll order the FFBI's luxury private jet service." She smiled. "I'll be able to take a little catnap and enjoy some caviar on the way."

CAVIAR?

"Just a joke, fish. Don't tell anyone, but you're making me rethink my diet." Ophelia sank onto her soft chaise longue and put her paws up behind her head. "A three-part heist! You know, this might be the trickiest job ever. Have I ever told you about the time, up in Alaska, when I—"

SMASH! CRASH! Without warning, a tennis ball came crashing through Ophelia's stained-glass skylight. Rainbow-colored shards were propelled into her living room. Ophelia looked at Oscar, startled. The doorbell rang, and he raced over to their security cameras.

"Hmm. Our system says it's the nosy neighbor dog, Thug, at the door." Oscar looked over at the clue. "But *do not* answer it until I can confirm with my innovative recognition tech that it's *actually* him," Oscar warned. "We have highly sensitive material in this room that nobody should see."

Ignoring him, Ophelia sauntered to the door. "Are you kidding me, fish? I bet Thug only has eyes for his slobbery toy! And I'm curious. I haven't met this mutt in person yet. We've just

been waving our paws at each other over the fence between our properties."

"Stop! The map! You can't open the door. It's ultra-top secret!"

But Ophelia already had her paw on the handle and was ready to come face-to-face with her next-door neighbor.

"Murphy's law says that anything that can go wrong, will go wrong. Murphy must have been a really bitter dog. Ophelia's law says to expect that everything will turn out beautifully."

—Ophelia von Hairball V

6

A SLY DOG

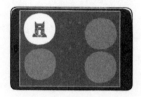

Behind Ophelia's back, a quick-thinking Oscar shouted, "P.U.G.! Vacuum! Now!" Without precise instructions of exactly where to vacuum, the robo-dog instantly sucked up anything that wasn't bolted down. Before Oscar could stop it, P.U.G. had pulled in the map, a very tall sandwich, a full bottle of Sapphire Spawrkle claw polish, and a diamond-encrusted mirror.

Holding on to his wig, Oscar yelled, "P.U.G. Stop vacuuming now!"

P.U.G. ceased its vacuum extravaganza, and Ophelia flung her front door open. "Well, hello there, neighbor! Come in, come in! I'm Ophelia. And this is Oscar, my fish-ssistant." The cat gestured around the room, which had been ravaged by P.U.G.'s impromptu windstorm. She turned her voice into a stage whisper. "As you can see, Oscar likes to break wind. He also enjoys dusting, so if you ever need extra help dusting doggy knickknacks over at your place, just ask." Oscar's fish face pinched with fury.

A tail-wagging, panting P.U.G. trotted to the door and sniffed Thug. Oscar straightened out his collar and tie. "And this," Oscar said, "is P.U.G."

"To be perfectly honest," Ophelia chimed in, "we're not really sure what it does." Oscar's tank started to bubble.

"Can you stay for tea?" Ophelia crooned. She didn't really have time for the mutt to come in, but she wanted to get a reaction out of Oscar. The fillet didn't disappoint.

OH. ER. WELL, HELLO THERE! **I'M THUG.**

YOU JUST LOOK **SO FAMILIAR**, OPHELIA. HAVE WE MET BEFORE?

HMM. I DON'T THINK SO.

OH DEAR. WELL, ANYHOW. I'M VERY SORRY ABOUT THIS **MESS!**

I WAS PLAYING FETCH—AND I'VE BEEN VERY CLUMSY.

I'M SO SORRY I BROKE YOUR WINDOW! DOGGONE IT, THIS PLACE IS **SWANKY.**

BUT I'M SURE YOU'RE BUSY. I WON'T KEEP YOU. PLEASE LET ME KNOW THE COST FOR **NEW GLASS** AND FOR THE CLEANUP!

Oscar looked at her and then to P.U.G. and started to shake. "Ophelia, I really don't think tea is a good idea," he muttered. But Thug bowed graciously to them both.

"Thanks for the invitation, but I'm so busy today with chores. Come over and play cards sometime?" He tipped his hat to them.

"Sounds lovely. I do enjoy a game of Go Fish." Ophelia waved good-bye to Thug. When he left, she shut the door, leaned against it, and then faced Oscar with a giant grin.

Oscar looked at the mess of glass and items around the room, put his fins on his hips, and shook his head. "That was *not ideal*, Ophelia! What were you thinking? We're on a high-security alert! You can't open this door, and you shouldn't be inviting strangers inside!" Oscar's attention was diverted for a moment by P.U.G., which was sniffing Thug's chewed-up, soggy, slobbery ball. The robo-dog had been programmed to perform over twenty dog-like actions. "Oh, yuck." Oscar shooed P.U.G. away from it. "Thug didn't even get his ball! Do you think I should take it over to him?"

"Don't touch that thing. It's really chewed up. The germs!" Ophelia shivered. "We'll need to decontaminate the place!" She stepped carefully around the broken glass and looked up. "Clumsy canine. I'd better take a peek."

Ophelia climbed up to the roof to check out the damage the dog had made.

"Wait for me!" With the help of his grappling hook, Oscar hooked onto the window frame and zipped up to join her. "I'll help clean. Hmm.

Maybe we should think about putting bars on the windows."

As Oscar surveyed the mess, Ophelia checked out the view, focusing on what was next door. "Oscar," she proclaimed, "we're going to have to do more than put bars on the windows." Her tail waved in the direction of Thug's yard. "*HISS.* Because that there, dear inventor, is a rather curious turn of events, wouldn't you say?"

Oh, Thug, you sly dog. This changes everything.

"When life tries to deliver you lemons, don't sign for them. Instead, hold out for the really sparkly packages."

—Ophelia von Hairball V

7

CAT ON A HOT TIN WOOF

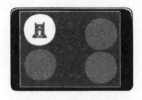

From the rooftop, Ophelia and Oscar stared down at Thug's yard. His shrubs were manicured in such a way that, from an aerial view, their formation of the CCIA symbol was undeniable.

Oscar's bulgy eyes rolled to the back of his head like he was going to faint. Ophelia helped him sit down. His voice was shaky. "This is outrageous! How dare Thug impersonate an innocent neighbor!"

The cat nodded. "Yes. Being next door is a rather good setup for him. It would have been smart for Thug to keep his CCIA identity under wraps, but those dogs always mark their territory. They can't help it." Her eyes narrowed. "Perhaps this arrangement could work to our advantage."

"Maybe we're just *seeing things* because we've got the CCIA on our brains. Perhaps our neighbor simply has overenthusiastic gardeners who like to make shapes in hedges!" Oscar said, hopeful that one of the FFBI's archenemies wasn't, in fact, living beside them.

Ophelia spoke with resolve. "We're not seeing things. Paris taught me not to underestimate those dogs." During her last big heist, the CCIA had almost trapped her in a mew-seum. Thankfully, her very quick wit allowed Ophelia to escape with considerable elegance.

In desperation, Oscar raised his fins. "Let's put this place up for sale and move!" he said. "I know a couple of great tropical locations. Seaside would

be lovely!" Ophelia could practically see his little gold head fill with watery dreams and schemes.

"Oh no. We're not moving anywhere. I love my cozy, fancy, *dry* lair." From the roof, she surveyed her neighborhood and tilted her head. "We'll deal with Thug later. My first priority is to get to Egypt. The FFBI jet will be ready for takeoff in thirty minutes. I need to study the Cairo Mewseum's blueprints. Please put together an array of gadgets for me to take—a kit of multipurpose tools would be fine and dandy." She smiled. "And I shall proudly wear my new cat burglar costume!"

Oscar's eyes bulged farther. He stood up tall

in his tank. "You're right. There's a lot to do. I'll get your burglar kit together. I'm including a new invention: an antiscent spray. It will cover up our—er—your scent, so if there are any dogs around, they won't be able to detect your presence. Is there anything else you'd like me to come up with? I'm feeling quite creative," Oscar told her.

"You know I don't like surprises," she reminded him. "Just the classic gadgets will be fabulous. As always, all my gear needs to fit in my gorgeous special-ops handbag."

Still on the lair's roof, Oscar removed his wig and tried to look extra smart, extra fast, and extra resourceful. (He'd been brushing up on his Inventor Academy 101 handbook.) He desperately hoped Ophelia would change her mind and invite him along on her important caper.

She didn't.

When they were back on the main floor, a clawful thought stopped Ophelia in her tracks. Her voice was low and slow. "Oscar, do you think it's a coincidence that Thug's ball, today of all days, smashed through your brand-new high-security measures?"

Oscar gasped, his mouth forming into the shape of a perfect bubble. "Oh!"

She put her paw in front of her mouth and signaled the fish to stay silent. Then, in a hiss-whisper, she advised, "There's more than a small chance that the ball is bugged. That shifty dog is probably listening to everything we say." Her eyes narrowed. "It seems like the purr-fect opportunity to take Thug and the rest of those CCIA mutts on a wild-goose chase."

"When you're caught between a rock and a hard place, make sure the rock is a diamond and the hard place is a purr-fectly planned escape route."

—Ophelia von Hairball V

8

GO, GO, GADGETY FISH

En route to Egypt, Ophelia used the flight time to try on a few new disguises, paint her claws, read a few (hilarious) books, brush up on her art history, check in with her FFBI contacts, and test out her new gadget kit.

When she landed, Ophelia breathed in the heat and the hiss-tory. She loved the country's

tradition of cat worship. *If only all cultures could be so smart.*

Mindful of Director MEW's reminder that she might be followed, Ophelia made several stops on the way to the Cairo Mew-seum and changed her disguises. Once she arrived, she stood in the courtyard, in front of a giant sphinx. It was magnificent.

PURRRR. PURRRR. It was the FFBI's secure line. "Where are you?" MEW asked.

"Egypt. And I'm certain," she informed the director, "that the first piece of the Scarlet Claw is somewhere in the Cairo Mew-seum. I'll have to do some investigating to figure out the exact location of where it was buried," she said. "Hopefully our FFBI contact here in Egypt can help with some information," she said.

"I hope so, too, Ophelia. Your inventor updated us about the CCIA member next door to your lair. Milton has a team there now to make sure everything's secure. I'm sure I don't need to tell you again that all the world's felines are depending on you to find the pieces of the Scarlet Claw first."

Normally filled with supreme confidence, Ophelia felt the tickle and tumble of nerves in her stomach. "No, ma'am. You don't have to tell me. I understand."

"Excellent. Remember, time is of the essence!"

Outside the Mew-seum, Everett, Ophelia's Egyptian FFBI contact, appeared. They sat together on a bench. Ophelia didn't waste a moment before questioning him. "What did you learn about this place?"

"Well," the contact whispered, "you asked for information from several years ago. I've learned there were three FFBI cat burglars in charge of hiding the three pieces of the Scarlet Claw laser pointer. One was an archaeologist who was interested in ancient Egypt. One was a theater buff from Canada. And one was a book lover who spent a lot of time in New York City."

ARCHAEOLOGIST
EGYPT

THEATER BUFF
CANADA

BOOK LOVER
NEW YORK

Though Ophelia appreciated the information, she didn't feel like she had enough intel to go on. "The clue I have," Ophelia told him, "led me here, to this museum. *If someone had to bury a massive piece of a machine here, where would they hide it? For example, was there anything special happening here around that time? Any new exhibits?*"

"I'm sorry," her contact confessed. "I wasn't

able to dig that deep in the short time I had. I'll keep searching and report back if I find anything. In the meantime, maybe there's a clue inside the Mew-seum? Good luck!"

Ophelia was alone.

Something unfamiliar gnawed away at Ophelia's insides. Normally, with every heist challenge she'd ever faced, she knew *exactly* what she was going after. Ophelia was an expert at making a winning strategy and purr-fect plans—with style, sass, and class to boot! But here and now, solo in the middle of Egypt, with a fast-ticking clock, Ophelia had no idea where she could find the first piece of the Scarlet Claw.

It's a big mew-seum. I can't just dig the whole thing up! But she knew she'd better figure out what to do—and fast.

What if I can't find it?

Ophelia knew that if she failed, a tarnished cat burglar reputation might not be the worst of her problems. If the CCIA had the first clue, it would only be a matter of time before those mutts also figured out that the first piece of the Scarlet Claw was at the Cairo Mew-seum.

And this time, Ophelia von Hairball V wasn't taking a trinket or treasure just for fun or to prove her legendary skills. She was taking something that *really* mattered to *a lot* of cats. Failure wasn't an option.

"They say imagination will get you everywhere.
But good accessories don't hurt."

—Ophelia von Hairball V

9

PAW-RTNERS IN CRIME

As she sat with her gorgeous claws over her fabulous face, Ophelia's cell phone started to **PURRRR** again. "How are you doing, paw-rtner?"

"We're not paw-rtners, Oscar," Ophelia said grumpily. "You don't even have paws."

"You're such a stickler for details," Oscar teased. "In any case, your unusually poor paw-sture tells me you might *need* a paw-rtner in crime. Of course, I'm here to help!"

"My paw-sture," the cat retorted, "is *impeccable*. And what does a flappy, floppy fish know about paw—?" She stopped. Her eyes narrowed. "Wait! How do you even know what I look like right now?!"

Unexpectedly, the fish inventor himself popped out from behind her. Oscar was sporting his S.P.I.T. and another new look. He held fast to his suitcase. "A good sidekick always knows when he or she is needed."

"How many times do I need to tell you, fish-flake—you're not a sidekick. You're my inventor. And I *don't* need you."

"I'm a *senior* inventor," he interjected.

"You're still on probation. While I appreciate your design skills and all the superior gear and gadgets you create, out in the field, *I work best by myself.*" Ophelia raised an eyebrow. "Also, great outfit."

Oscar nodded at her compliment, his expression serious. "So this 'by yourself' thing—how's that working out for you right now?" he inquired. There was a small edge to his normally upbeat voice. "I only ask because this particular mission is rather difficult, not to mention *the most important one you've ever been on.* And since you're still sitting here on this bench and not stealing *anything* at all, I'm going to assume you actually *need* my help."

Ophelia was both shocked and fur-ious that her inventor (who should have been home doing official fishy things) was with her in Cairo. But at this desperate moment, she couldn't deny that Oscar was right. She could use all the brains he was offering.

"Okay, okay. But just so you know, I'm *very* mad! How did you get here so fast?"

He smiled. "I flew. *I* actually flew *you* here. And you didn't even notice." He pulled out his tablet and showed her the selfies of him in the FFBI jet. Ophelia looked at his pictures.

"There's no time for a hiss-y fit. Let's get down

to business. Your FFBI research friend was right about the three cat burglars who hid the three pieces of the laser pointer. But he wasn't able to access all the databases I hacked—er . . . *found*."

"Let me tell you about those three old FFBI cats who stole the Scarlet Claw and hid the pieces. They were elite, top-ranking cats with excellent reputations. One was based here in Egypt and was in charge of all the Cairo Mew-seum's operations. The second was in Vancouver—she was a theater buff who spent most of her time on Granville Street downtown. The third was from New York—a well-known patron of the big public library." Oscar stopped and adjusted his hat. "I'm betting that when we find this first piece, the new clue will point us to one of those cities."

"Okay. But we need to find the first piece. Was there anything special going on *here* at the time the FFBI agent had to hide the Scarlet Claw? Any events or construction?"

"As a matter of fact," he said with a smile, "they were building this very courtyard at the time the device was hidden."

Ophelia's eyes popped open. "And the FFBI agent probably would have done what *any* of us would do when hiding something important. . . ."

Oscar finished her thought: ". . . He would have tried to leave some kind of clue!"

With natural stealth (Stealth was actually her middle name), Ophelia climbed a tree and surveyed the courtyard.

"Oscar," she divulged with a grin, "indeed, our cat left a rather gorgeous clue—" But before she could say anything else, an alarm sounded and Oscar's fins flapped.

"Oh no!" he cried. "I planted several canine

sensors around the mew-seum. That alarm means there is a higher than normal concentration of dogs in the area. We've got company! Let's find somewhere to hide while we figure out how we're going to dig out this device."

Ophelia pounced to the ground. "I wish we had time to formulate a thoughtful plan. But we need to get rid of those dogs—quickly. Go on, fish—do something crazy. The dogs will start chasing you and then I'll extract these stones."

Oscar didn't move. "I want you to know that under any normal set of circumstances, I would nod my head repeatedly and agree with every single thing you said. You are, after all, the best cat burglar on the entire planet. Probably off the planet, too. But *you* digging up rocks is the most ridiculous plan I've ever heard. What about your manicure?"

"It's not an ideal solution," she conceded, "but do you have something better in mind? Are you planning on flipping stones over with your delicate gold tail?"

"As a matter of fact, I happen to know something that can out-dig the both of us."

Before Ophelia could register what Oscar was saying, he opened his suitcase, took out a sleek remote, flipped a few switches, and made a lot of fin-fare about pressing the gold button that was smack in the middle.

From out of the bush, P.U.G. appeared. "Ta-da!" the robo-dog exclaimed in Oscar's voice.

Ophelia opened her mouth, but no words came out.

"I'll instruct P.U.G. to dig up those rocks. Then I'll hide in the bushes and be the lookout. Meanwhile, you can create a purr-fect diversion. As soon as those dogs see you, they'll chase you."

Ophelia didn't want to admit that his plan was genius. (What she really wanted was to unplug P.U.G.) Un-fur-tunately, she had no choice but to go along with Oscar's purr-posterous idea and allow the caper-crashing robo-dog abomination to dig to its metal heart's content.

"Just please don't get caught," Oscar warned Ophelia.

Ophelia forgot her agitation, laughed, and put on her cat burglar suit. "Oh, my dear Oscar. I've made an art out of *never* getting caught."

In the mew-seum, Ophelia gave the CCIA dogs the chase of their lives. She was just pouncing down from a sphinx when Oscar's voice was in her ear. "Er—can you please return to the court-yard?" Oscar's tight whisper was a sign of stress.

"Oh no! Did you get yourself fish-napped again?" she asked.

"No," he responded. "But we do have a . . . different sort of situation. Please meet me behind the bench," he advised.

Other than Oscar seeming a tad disheveled, things looked fine to Ophelia. "Wow, I gave them

SLAM!

a good chase. Are you done?" She surveyed the scene, noting the dug hole and an empty space in the dirt. "You found it! What happened to your outfit?" she asked.

He straightened his hat. "I had a fight with a shrub. I lost." He took a deep breath. "So, yes. The good news is that P.U.G. dug up the courtyard stones like a bot-boss and found the first piece of the Scarlet Claw."

"Excellent." Ophelia's eyes twinkled. "What is it?"

Oscar's head drooped. "Well, it's a base of some kind. Looks to be a power source. But . . ." He blinked quickly. "There is some very, very *bad* news. I instructed P.U.G. to dig up the device and clue and then to only give them to me. And now . . ." He gulped. "Well, now the device and the clue are gone! I definitely gave P.U.G. accurate instructions. I'm not sure what happened. Maybe it short-circuited?"

"HISS!" Anger surged through Ophelia and her fur stood on end. "One of those doggone miserable mutts must have nabbed it!" she exclaimed. She frowned at P.U.G., which was oblivious to her fury, but then took a deep breath. She knew a tantrum directed at a well-meaning fish or a pile of bolts would do nothing but eat up precious time. "We have no time to fret, fish. I have a policy against being late or losing. These dogs may be book-smart, but they lack our street savvy. There is always hope. We'll find a way to get this piece back and get the next piece—fast."

"If you're going to be diabolical, do it with a dash of diva and a lot of twinkle."

—Ophelia Stealth von Hairball V

10

CLUELESS IN CAIRO

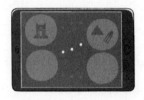

Watching P.U.G. mindlessly chase a butterfly gave Ophelia an idea. "As usual, I just had a rather superior thought," she told Oscar.

"I'm all ears," he responded.

"Do you even have ears?"

"Yes. They're just different than yours."

"Let's not dwell on the super-fish-al stuff. The faux pooch has a camera, no?"

"Are you talking about P.U.G.?"

"What do you think I'm talking about?"

Oscar's annoyance turned into happiness when he realized what Ophelia was thinking. "Of course!" He called P.U.G. and removed a microchip.

"If we're lucky, the P.U.G. cam has captured exactly what happened after P.U.G. dug up the base of the Scarlet Claw. Maybe those CCIA mutts read the map out loud and we'll know exactly where to go from here! We'll meet up with them at the next spot, steal back the first piece, get the second piece, and find the map for the last piece! It's all going to be fine, fish."

Oscar plugged P.U.G.'s camera chip into his tablet and watched the small screen with anticipation as they played back P.U.G.'s digging frenzy. They saw P.U.G. carefully extract the Scarlet Claw base with a magnet. Then they held their breath in anticipation of seeing dogs enter the picture.

But to their surprise, the P.U.G. cam didn't pick up *any* CCIA members. Instead, a very furmiliar unibrow showed up.

Why was Pierre in Egypt? And why was he steal-ing the very clue he had been ordered to help Ophelia nab?!

"Wow!" Oscar exclaimed. "This isn't what I was expecting!" His eyes grew a bit bulgier, and he frowned. "He must have followed us here! This goes against what MEW told all the cat burglars. *You* were the only cat who was supposed to get the Scarlet Claw pieces!"

"Yes. I wish I had time to throw a good tantrum about it," Ophelia said, "but we need to solve this." She put her face closer to the footage. "Oscar, does

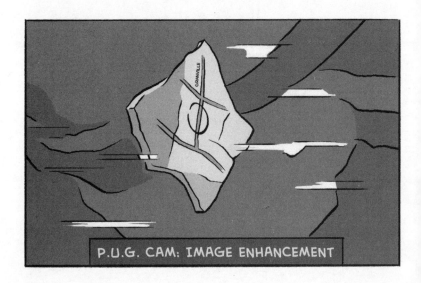

P.U.G. CAM: IMAGE ENHANCEMENT

the P.U.G. cam zoom? Can we get a better look at the map?"

Oscar jumped into action. "Of course. P.U.G. has the highest-quality camera."

Ophelia examined the map and smiled. "Purr-fect! We're going to Canada," she said. "Now there's a place after my own good-mannered heart!"

"There are several older theaters in the Vancouver area where the old FFBI agent used to work." Oscar sighed. "Should we just go to each one and hunt for clues?"

"There's no need," Ophelia said, pointing at the map. "See the O?"

Oscar's face broke into a grin. "The Orpheum Theater! It's an omen! Get it? O-men?! O-rpheum!"

"That's right, fish. We'll head there now."

"'We'?! You mean you're letting me come to Vancouver? And P.U.G., too?"

"I don't have much choice," Ophelia said dryly. "Since you ditched my pilot back at home, you're in charge of the flight."

Oscar saluted. "We won't fish-appoint you!"

"Umbrella, please?" From the damp airport in Vancouver, the trio took the SkyTrain downtown to Granville Station.

When they arrived, Ophelia looked around. "The tricky part of this," she told Oscar, "is that Pierre won't be trying to lose the CCIA. He's just not that careful. He'll race here, and those dogs will happily follow him. So keep your big eyes open for mutts and a unibrow."

At the Orpheum, the doors were locked. Oscar looked at Ophelia. "How do we get in?"

"Elementary, my fish." She pointed a paw half-way up the building. "I'm going to jump up and check those windows. If they're secure, I'll use an old-fashioned method to gain entrance." She showed Oscar her jeweled claw file.

"We can't come in with you?" Oscar asked.

"Absolutely not." There was no wiggle room in her voice. "I need you to be my lookout."

Without waiting for his agreement, Ophelia pounced up onto the awning and disappeared. Oscar put his hands on his fish-hips and addressed P.U.G. "Just between you and me, that cat sometimes makes me want to have a good, loud fish-fit!" P.U.G. nodded sympathetically. Because it'd been coded by a treat-loving inventor fish, the robot produced seaweed snacks for Oscar to make him feel better. Just as Oscar was about to indulge, he heard several short barks. Up the street was a dapper-looking dog pack sporting shiny CCIA badges.

"Fish sticks! We need to hide," Oscar whispered to P.U.G. "Let's crash Ophelia's party and go into the theater. Be as quiet as possible."

"Sometimes you move one pounce forward
and two pounces back. Only do that
when the treasure is behind you."

—Ophelia von Hairball V

11

LIGHTS, CAMERA, HAIRBALL ACTION!

From the window, Ophelia pounced into the dark lobby and whistled with awe. With the help of her ultrapowerful flashlight, she was able to appreciate how grand the theater's lobby was.

She slid through elegant, gold archways and opened a set of double doors. Inside the theater, she stood at the top of the stairs and looked down at the rows and rows of velvet seats. A bright spotlight captured the sparkle of a massive chandelier. She felt right at home. For a moment, she imagined it filled with audience members in beautiful outfits.

She thought back to the clue that P.U.G. captured on camera and a Cheshire cat's smile formed across her face. The image on the second map had looked like a light fixture. Light fixture, Orpheum Theater . . . It took Ophelia's sophisticated feline mind no time at all to put the hints together. *This*, she thought, *is such a clever hiding place for a piece like that. Nobody would ever notice an extra fixture hanging from the ceiling. Maybe it even works?*

She went down the stairs to the stage and felt a shiver crawl up her back. *Is someone watching me?*

Without warning, all the stage lights went from dark to blindingly bright. Before her, at center stage, all spotlights moved to focus on her cousin and archenemy—*Pierre*! Ophelia also noted the shadow of Norman, Pierre's small, shifty, amphibious inventor.

"No, you're not," Ophelia chided, trying to remain calm.

Pierre laughed maniacally. It echoed through the theater. "You are just an overblown, overrated, fancy ball of fluff."

Ophelia felt an angry prickle, but she knew she should stay focused. She inched closer to the stage as he continued to rant. He cleared his throat and smoothed his unibrow. "You were a bit too late getting here. *I've already found* the second piece. It's a magnifier of some sort. With it, of course, was the third clue."

He stuck out his tongue and continued. "Norman! Move one of the spotlights to show Ophelia the pieces!" In an instant, the bright light exposed two large pieces of the Scarlet Claw behind Pierre on stage. "They're mine!" His voice shifted from excited to menacing.

Norman, the frog inventor, cleared his throat. Pierre paused. "Oh. Also, I want to just mention that Norman's *very* useful. I'm glad you rejected him. He knows technology—and he's artistic, too.

The fish mask he constructed to get the first piece of the device was genius."

He stared her down, his black eyes flat without any twinkle at all. "So now I have two pieces of the Claw, and I'm the only one who knows where to find the last piece. *And you don't.*"

AND ONCE I GET THE LAST PIECE, I'LL HAVE ALL THE POWER.

Ophelia's heart beat faster. "Get real, Pierre. Even if you manage to somehow pull this off, you aren't going to be the number-one FFBI cat burglar. The basic principles of honor and purr-fection are beyond you. You might get one tiny moment in the spotlight, but that's it. Because I'll always outclass you. And if your plan is to prove to Director MEW that you're better than me, you should know that she'll be fur-ious, because you didn't follow her instructions."

Pierre produced a sinister smile. Then he stepped forward to the edge of the stage and loomed directly above her. He was backlit by a massive spotlight, and a grotesquely dark Pierre shadow stretched all around her. "Director MEW? *Who said anything about giving this to her?*"

Ophelia felt a hiss leave her body and leaned on the stage to steady herself. *Is he planning to betray the FFBI?*

"Ophelia, for such a mastermind, you're so naïve. Don't you understand? Once I have all three pieces of the Scarlet Claw and put the giant laser pointer into action, I won't need *you*, I won't need *MEW*, and I won't need the *FFBI*."

"Dance like everyone's watching.
And do extra twirls."

—Ophelia von Hairball V

12

DOUBLE CAT-CROSS

Ophelia couldn't believe what she was hearing. Pierre was planning on double-crossing everyone to get the Scarlet Claw! He wanted to control *all the cats.*

"I'm tired of all of you and your old-fashioned ways," Pierre ranted. "When I'm in charge, I'll get rid of everything classic." His eyes lit up. "Maybe I'll make my own agency and fill it with burglars who don't care about classic capers or useless traditions. We won't focus on the art of burglary. We'll just steal whatever we want! And we won't give stuff back, either!" His smile got more sinister. "Maybe I'll call it Purr-fect Pierre's Steal-Everything Academy."

"P.P.S.E.A.? Not a smart name!" P.U.G. marched down the ramp toward the stage, its voice carrying through the theater.

Oscar popped out from the front-row seat he'd been hiding behind and leaned in to whisper to Ophelia. "How about this new P.U.G. voice, Ophelia?" he asked, hoping to direct attention away from the fact that they weren't supposed to be inside the theater.

"This *may not be the right time* for P.U.G. voice auditions," she hiss-whispered back, tight-lipped. "Why are you even in here? You're supposed to be outside, keeping watch for the dogs!"

"The CCIA is on its way. The dogs are just up the street," he informed her, out of breath. "Plus I really, really wanted to see what was happening."

"Speak up, you two!" Pierre shouted. "*I'm* the star of this show. And the director! And I didn't give you *any lines*!" His shadow waved furiously.

Ophelia ignored her egomaniacal cousin. "The situation here is quite dire," she told Oscar, her voice low. "Did you hear what Pierre said?"

"You mean how he has two pieces of the Scarlet Claw device and that he has the only clue to find the third piece? And how he's going to try to take over the world? Yes, indeed. This is better than fiction!" he said. Ophelia scowled. "I mean, it's much, much worse than fiction!"

Barking sounds wafted into the theater. The dogs were close. "I'm so sorry to interrupt your little conversation," Pierre said, "but Norman and I have to go get the third piece of the Scarlet Claw." He grabbed his inventor by the collar and climbed up the curtain toward the rooftop. "See ya. Wouldn't wanna be ya." He waved. "Oh! And don't bother following us," he sneered. "That fancy-shmancy FFBI jet you flew in on sprang a fuel leak. You won't be using it any time soon."

WOOF! Pierre disappeared, but the dogs were closing in. Ophelia crawled into a front-row seat.

"Outrageous," she fumed. "Pierre has lost his marbles. Also, did you see my Captain Claw-some action figure?! *Pierre sewed a unibrow on him!*"

Oscar's head was in his fins. "Forget Captain Claw-some. We've got to get out of here before the dogs find us. We better call MEW and tell her Pierre is planning to take over the entire universe!"

"Oh, my dear fish-flake." Ophelia shook her head. She hopped up on stage, grabbed a top hat and cane from a pile of costumes in the corner, and did a little tap dance. "Pierre will do nothing of the sort. He wouldn't even know what to steal if MEW didn't give him a list. Besides, he'll just say he was on stage *acting*. No, we just have to get our paws and fins on the pieces he has."

"And the last one, too!" Oscar looked at her.

"Of course, of course," she said.

P.U.G. began to pant.

Ophelia twirled around on stage like the professional dancer she was.

"Please disable that ridiculous voice function on your metal abomination immediately," Ophelia said to Oscar, "or I will."

But before Oscar could react, the back door of the theater burst open and light cast down the central aisle. With a fast, graceful swoop worthy of all the most legendary cat burglars, Ophelia did a silent roll off stage left. "Oscar, kill the lights!" In a flash, out came his retractable antigravity hook. He aimed it at the light switches and hit them dead-on. The theater was black.

"Orchestra pit," Ophelia whispered. Oscar and P.U.G. followed her silently.

"Tap the side of your mask," said Oscar. "Trust me!"

She had no choice but to do what Oscar said. Suddenly, she could see purr-fectly in the dark.

"A small bonus with the cat burglar mask. That *particular* gold button tells your mask to adjust to the conditions. Sensing the darkness, it's produced a small see-in-the-dark film over your eyes. Like really smart sunglasses. And you should see what happens when—"

Ophelia cut him off. "Oscar! Our pesky next-door neighbor is leading the pack of paw-and-order mutts!"

Oscar gasped. "Thug? Really? Oh no! This is *not* fin-tastic. What are we going to do?"

The cat looked him in the eyes. "We, dear fish, are going to New York. We know the final piece of the Scarlet Claw is there. Then we're going to stop Pierre and prove, once again, that I'm the best cat burglar in the world. We'll deal with our devious dog neighbor later."

Oscar asked, "How do we know it's in New York?"

"Remember the three FFBI agents who originally hid the clues? They were located in Cairo, Vancouver, and ..."

"New York City!" the fish cheered.

Ophelia and Oscar didn't have much, but they had their brains ... and each other. *Would that be enough?*

"Never leave home without impeccable manners, unrelenting grit, and a slab of fine chocolate."

—Ophelia von Hairball V

13

OLD-FASHIONED FABULOUS

With the help of Vancouver FFBI allies, Oscar and Ophelia quickly secured a new jet to take them to New York City. It wasn't as opulent as their last one, but it was just as fast.

Oscar was trying a new disguise. "I'm going for the aviator look," he explained.

"Love it." Ophelia nodded. "But you're really

going to have to put some good, strong fasteners on the sides of that S.P.I.T. glass," she advised. "Crooked hair is a pet peeve of mine." She unfolded the silhouetted picture of the three original FFBI thieves and studied them.

Oscar's voice shook with concern. "This is a really long shot, but if we want to beat Pierre, we'll have to research more about the third FFBI agent. All we know right now is that he liked the New York Public Library. Let's find out everything we can about the cat who hid the final piece of the Scarlet Claw!" He blinked a few times. "The thing is, it might take a while. We don't even have a name." Oscar held up his fin. "I could start by cross-checking FFBI records with library patrons—"

Ophelia cut him off. "No cross-checking necessary." She flicked her tail and squinted at the picture. "I may have, at one point in my career, been a fan of the former elite cat burglars. Their old-fashioned skills were amazing, of course."

Ophelia's memory sparked and she snapped

her claws together. "Our New York connection is Isaac! He was one of the most ingenious cat burglars the world has ever seen."

Oscar handed Ophelia a laptop. "As a classic cat, I know you'd rather do your research in a library, but this is all we've got right now." He was firm. "You use this. I'll use the tablet. Maybe we'll learn enough about Isaac to figure out where he hid the last piece!"

Simultaneously, Oscar and Ophelia typed

away, trying to discover any detail they could about FFBI cat burglar Isaac.

After almost an hour of diving into rabbit holes, Ophelia finally lifted her head up. "Oh, wow," she exclaimed and looked at her finned accomplice. "The old cat's alive. And still in New York!" She smiled and showed Oscar her findings. "Please contact him, explain our situation, and ask him to meet us the moment we land! And if the last piece is somewhere in the Big Apple, we'll need transportation. Arrange that, too. Make it a luxury helicopter. It's not often I get an unlimited budget!"

Oscar frowned. "We don't have time for an in-person meeting. Let's just call. Pierre is probably already in New York."

"A face-to-face meeting is much nicer than a phone call. As for Pierre . . ." Ophelia reached into her handbag and pulled out a device. "Check this out, fish."

Oscar grabbed the device and peered at its screen. He let out a surprised squawk.

143

Ophelia chuckled.

"According to the tracker, we have at least an hour before he lands in New York. We might be able to find the last piece before him!"

When they touched down, Oscar was smiling. "Isaac is here. He's excited to meet with us."

On the tarmac, the trio was greeted by an ancient FFBI cat. His voice was growly, but he had a mischievous twinkle in his eye. Ophelia sensed his kindness and sharp intelligence.

"I hear the two of you are short on time," Isaac said. "I didn't want to transmit any sensitive information online or via phone. In person is more secure. It's the way we used to do things."

"I," Ophelia gushed, "am a *very, very* big fan of how you used to do things. Sometimes I wish the world could go back to times like that."

"Really?" Isaac laughed. "Sometimes I wish I'd had a bit more technology when I was in the field. It sure would have made things a lot easier!"

Even though nobody else was near, Ophelia's voice dropped to a whisper. "We found the base for the Scarlet Claw in Egypt and the magnifier in Canada." She didn't mention that they didn't actually *have* them. "What can you tell us about the last piece?" Ophelia asked. "Where is it?"

"Are you familiar with the New York Public Library?" Isaac asked.

Ophelia nodded. "Somewhat."

"It's there." Isaac brightened up. "Do you know the story about how it all happened? About how we stole the Scarlet Claw from the CCIA right out from under their super-duper dog noses? About how we had to split it up?"

Ophelia looked at him with curiosity. "We were given only the short version." Oscar was hopping up and down, doing an impatient fish dance (which resembled the chicken dance), but Ophelia's inquiring cat mind got the best of her. She glanced at the Pierre-tracker. He wouldn't land for another thirty minutes or so. "We'd be honored if you could fill us in."

"It was many, many moons ago. The FFBI was so happy when the three of us intercepted the Scarlet Claw from the CCIA. We were young, elite cat burglars back then. We all had a whole lotta cat-itude. We snuck it off their carrier plane right here on this very tarmac! I was pretty stealthy in those days. Our task was to deliver the device to the original FFBI HQ in New York's Flatiron Building. But then we got word from our director that CCIA presence was heavy! Even back then, those dogs were no laughing matter. We decided to split the device up and find safe places to hide the pieces. I had the last piece. I managed to get past those dogs and make it uptown to the library, where I worked. My cohort cats jumped into two different planes and flew away with the pieces! One cat took the base to Egypt, and the other got the magnifier to Canada. They hid them there with encrypted maps. Your Director MEW kept the map to where the base was for all these years." Isaac paused to look at Oscar and Ophelia. They were captivated by his story. (P.U.G. was eyeing a mosquito and drooling.)

"Meow! That must have been a thrilling caper! So your piece is at the New York Public Library?" Ophelia asked. "The main building?"

"Sure is. That ruby was *so* heavy, but—"

Ophelia fluffed her tail. "A *ruby*?"

"Yes." Isaac got a nostalgic glint in his eyes. "And I'm telling you, the ruby that can power the Scarlet Claw is the largest, clearest, most beautiful jewel I've ever set my eyes upon—also, it's potentially the most dangerous if it gets hooked up with the Scarlet Claw base and the magnifier! The night I hid it, I plopped it into a burlap sack and then carried it up to the library's attic. I found an old box to hide it in. I marked it—"

"—*Odds and Ends*?" Ophelia interrupted.

Isaac and Oscar looked at her in surprise. "Why, yes," Isaac said. "You know about that?"

Ophelia blinked. "Everyone knows! It's an urban legend. I've been hearing rumors about a giant gem boxed in an attic for years. I can't believe it's true. I can't believe it's at the library!"

The old cat smiled. "Well, it's true. And that's where it is." He looked at his pocket watch. "But I suppose you two don't have time for ancient stories delivered by an old cat. Get going! Find the ruby! Save the world!"

Ophelia thanked Isaac, then hurried to the FFBI helicopter Oscar had ordered. "To the library!" Oscar commanded. He was thrilled to be part of this heist. "Ophelia?"

"Hmm," she said, deep in thought.

"This chopper's really fancy. But since we won't be able to order luxury choppers on most of our heists, when we get back, would you let me design a really cool vehicle for us? I can craft something fast and sleek! It'll have the most sophisticated gadgets! Maybe I'll make it match your cat burglar suit . . . or I'll design it so you can change its color—to match your mood!"

"I'd consider having a custom vehicle," she agreed, "if it could be *exactly* like James Bond's Aston Martin DB5."

"Similar." Oscar nodded. "But I'd make better gadgets."

As they flew to the library, Ophelia looked out the window and smiled at her reflection in the mirror. *This*, she thought, *is paws-down going to be the most interesting heist of my career to date.*

"When in doubt, add twenty percent more sparkle."

—Ophelia von Hairball V

14

PATIENCE PLUS FUR-TITUDE

At the big New York Public Library building, Oscar set up P.U.G.'s canine detection alarms with some precise instructions: "Please run at an exact speed of ten miles per hour around the perimeter of the library. Do not collide with anything or anyone. At one-hundred-foot intervals, lay these sensors down. We've got to stick together after this, so find me when you're finished. Go!"

"Excellent," Ophelia said. "We already have a tracker on Pierre. Now we'll know when the dogs get here, too."

Ophelia admired the lion statues on the front steps. "One is called Patience." Oscar pointed. "The other is Fortitude."

"We need both today."

Just as Ophelia was about to curtsy in front of the lions, she heard a sound like a spray, then felt a wet mist settle on her. Because getting wet was on her list of top-five "things to avoid at all costs," she let out a mighty growl.

"Oops! No need to get your claws out," Oscar admonished. "I just sprayed us both with my new antiscent spray invention. It should cover our scents while we're in the library. We don't want those dogs to sniff us out!"

Ophelia's nose twitched double time and her eyes squinted tight. "While I *want* to praise your fin-tastic foresight and fabulous fish brain, I must ask . . . *why do I smell like SEAWEED?!*"

"Just trying different things," he said, slightly

sheepish. "I can do pepperoni-scented next time if you want."

Ophelia sighed, curtsied to each of the lion statues, and flipped her tail back and forth a few times as she walked up the stairs to try and rid herself of the smell.

Oscar leaned closer to her. "I'm so excited that I can hardly stand it. I *can't wait* to hear the plan," he said. "How are we going to get the ruby?"

"When did I say that?"

"In last month's *Al Jazzycat* interview."

"Did I?" Ophelia was slightly a-mew-sed by how much of a fan-fish her inventor was.

"Absolutely. I've memorized key statements of yours," he told her. "They help me design better things for you. Trust me, Ophelia. I know you're not confident yet about having me come on heists with you, but you'll be hooked on me and my designs soon! And speaking of design ..."

"Um ... were we speaking of design?" Ophelia asked.

"Well, not really," he said sheepishly. "But I was wondering how you like the cat burglar suit so far?"

Ophelia pulled back the collar of her jacket to reveal a bit of the cat burglar suit underneath. "So far, so grand! I anticipate it will help me make a fast and anonymous getaway!" she said.

"I need to tell you about the special gadgets I designed for that suit," he cautioned. "All those buttons do different things. For example—"

"We really don't have time now," Ophelia shushed him. "We'll do a tutorial when we're home."

P.U.G. returned and Oscar looked at it. "We need to stick together."

They walked inside, entering the main entryway of the library—Astor Hall. Ophelia turned to Oscar, serious. "Can you please check Pierre's location? And from this moment on, it's absolutely imperative that I know where he is. The dogs will be close behind him."

Oscar's little gold head swiveled as he scanned the room. Seeing nothing suspicious, he checked the Pierre-tracker. "He's just down the block!" His eyes narrowed. "Norman will be by his side."

"I would bet my inventor that the CCIA dogs are very close behind *them*." Ophelia gestured that they sit on one of the benches where she could keep an eye out for anyone coming in.

"What do you mean *you'd bet your inventor*? I'm your inventor!"

"Scale your anger, fish. I'm mostly joking."

"While you get the ruby, P.U.G. and I will keep an eye out," Oscar said. "Actually . . . now that we have P.U.G., I could put *it* on alert, then I could come with you to the attic! We could find that *Odds and Ends* box as a team and get the ruby *together*!"

"No," Ophelia answered with conviction. "That's not the plan." With a single claw, Ophelia beckoned him to move closer to her. "*The plan* is that you're the lookout until you hear my next instructions. *I'm* going to get the ruby. Then we're going to get the base and magnifier from Pierre. Finally, we'll head to FFBI HQ and deliver the Scarlet Claw pieces to MEW! Let's do this!" She pounced up from the bench and tapped her ear-piece. "You'll be hearing from me."

"Pierre and Norman are in front of the building," Oscar reported. "And right behind them are the CCIA dogs. A whole pack of them! I don't think Pierre knows he's being followed."

"Of course he doesn't. He's such a sloppy burglar. And I'll bet he's been blabbing about where the ruby is, too. That means I'm going to have a lot of company up in this attic very soon. From

where you are, can you see if Pierre has the first two Scarlet Claw pieces with him?" Ophelia asked.

"Pierre doesn't have the pieces," Oscar said. He didn't really want to mention to her that Pierre was clutching her Captain Claw-some action figure.

Ophelia frowned. *Where are the other two pieces of the Scarlet Claw device?*

"Newton's third law says that every action
has an equal and opposite reaction. So
pounce boldly and sparkle hard."

—Ophelia von Hairball V

15

CLAW-STROPHOBIC

Ophelia's voice was shrill through Oscar's ear-piece. "Where are the pieces we have to deliver to the FFBI?"

Oscar took a deep breath, knowing Ophelia wasn't going to like what he had to say. "Well," Oscar began, "I'm not sure where the device pieces are, but I should let you know that Pierre is carrying your Captain Claw-some action figure.

Its new, handcrafted unibrow is as impressive as his own. May I just say I think it's *slightly* odd that he carries that thing around wherever he goes? But I guess I'm not one to judge. After all, I had a security blanket and a small, orange-haired troll I used for good luck—"

"Oscar!" Ophelia interrupted. Her voice was tight. "Stop nattering about security blankets and trolls! You know perfectly well how I feel about my action figure. I want it back. As a matter of fact, I *need* it back."

"I think it would be safe to assume," Oscar informed Ophelia, "that the pieces of the Scarlet Claw are in Pierre's plane. So after you bring down the ruby, we can go get them on our way to FFBI HQ."

"Hmm. It's never a good idea to assume anything," Ophelia told Oscar. She sighed. "So many challenges, so little time. Is Norman carrying anything?"

"Norman has something like a book?" Oscar confirmed. "But not any devices. He's got a silver tray, too. Pierre is snacking. That is one high-maintenance kitty."

Ophelia was concerned that she didn't know for sure where the Scarlet Claw pieces were. "Okay. I'm coming down." But a loud P.U.G. *snort* through the communication device gave her a strange (yet amazing) idea.

"Cancel that." Ophelia's voice became crisp with authority. "Oscar, this is the time for your gold to shine. I need to stay up here a bit longer and extract some information from Pierre."

PLEASE CREATE A REASON FOR PIERRE TO TAKE THE **ELEVATOR**, AND **DETAIN NORMAN** ON THE MAIN FLOOR.

"What? Why? How? You have the ruby! We need to go!"

"You need to learn that being an elite, classic cat burglar means covering all your bases. In this case, I want to know where all the pieces of the Scarlet Claw are before we leave this library."

"What? How? I'll *never* be able to separate Norman and Pierre. Norman is a *dedicated* inventor who won't leave his cat burglar's side. And that's how it should be!" Oscar exclaimed.

"Getting Pierre in the elevator should be easy: He's lazy and hates the stairs. As for Norman, you know that little ribbit-giblet better than I do. I'm sure you'll figure out how to divert him."

Oscar's brain was moving a mile a minute. "Okay. Let's say Pierre gets on the elevator and I manage to detain Norman. *Then what?*"

"Then cut the communication channels between those two and find a way to get that elevator very, very stuck," she said. "I've got the *Odds and Ends* box! Now I just have to get Pierre to tell me where he stashed his Scarlet Claw pieces."

The inventor's bulgy eyes blinked. "Okay. At least I get to tinker with an elevator. Finally, a chance to use my IQ the way it was meant to be used, paw-rtner!"

"I never said we were paw-rtners," Ophelia retorted as a reflex.

"We're a dynamic duo! You and me! Oscar and Ophelia! O2. Oh! Did I mention I made a—"

Ophelia interrupted. "Focus, fish! I'm in the elevator maintenance room. Also, I need P.U.G. up here on the double. And keep your mic on, because I have a few very important instructions coming."

"P.U.G.? Did you just say you *need* P.U.G.?"

"Yes. Send it to the top of the elevator, please."

Just for giggles, Oscar dialed up the bot's panting and drooling features. "Thirteen-percent-more-authentic dog coming just for you, Ophelia!"

"Are we good to go, fillet?" Ophelia questioned.

"Yes. P.U.G. is on its way up to meet you. And I'm ready, too," Oscar confirmed. "Pierre and Norman just came into the library. My mission: a Norman distraction! And once Pierre is in the elevator, it *will* get stuck." The fish smiled. "*Guaranteed.*"

Norman's face changed from green to red, and he stomped off, huffing, toward the elevator. Oscar contacted Ophelia. "Okay, cat. Pierre is in the elevator. It's stuck. Norman is down here fuming." His voice turned to a whisper. "I see the CCIA, Ophelia! The dog pack, led by Thug, is now inside the library."

"Okay," Ophelia responded. "P.U.G. and I have a quick job to do. What I need you to do now is give P.U.G. *Norman's voice*."

"Oh! So you *like* our robot's voice feature now? You want me to turn P.U.G. into a ribb-bot?!" Oscar laughed at his own joke, then went into P.U.G.'s program via his tablet and altered the code. "Ophelia, you are fortunate that I still have reference files for Norman's voice from a few of his old presentations at the FFBI Inventor Academy." His fins flew expertly over his screen as he moved files around. "Voice programming complete. To activate it, simply whisper the command 'speak' and then say what you want P.U.G. to say. It'll repeat what you say in Norman's voice."

Ophelia jumped into the elevator shaft from a doorway in the maintenance room and met P.U.G. on top of the stuck elevator. She could hear the CCIA dogs who had already made it to the Rose Reading Room. Thanks to Oscar's antiscent spray, all traces of Ophelia were obliterated, and the dogs weren't able to sniff her out. Ophelia could hear Thug. With a calm command, he directed his CCIA crew to the attic.

Ophelia was surprised that Thug sounded exceptionally *classy*. "Whatever you do," he ordered his crew, "do *not* make a mess. Leave everything as you found it. There are some very old, very important historic things here—one of which must be the last piece of the Scarlet Claw. Our intel says it's in a box marked *Odds and Ends*."

Ophelia knew it wouldn't take the dogs long before they figured out that the box they wanted was missing, so she turned her attention back to Pierre, stuck in the elevator below her, to try to get the information she needed.

"Ugh, still stuck in the elevator," Pierre ranted into his earpiece. Since Oscar had cut his communication channel to Norman, he was actually just ranting to himself.

Ophelia started whispering words to P.U.G. to repeat to Pierre.

"But you *never* want to take the stairs," P.U.G. said in Norman's voice.

Ophelia was very impressed—P.U.G. sounded *exactly* like Norman.

"You sound close, Norman. Where are you? Can you see me? I demand you get me out of here at once!"

"I'm working on it. In the meantime, should I grab the Scarlet Claw pieces and bring them to the library?"

"Why on earth would you do *that*, frog?! Nobody's going to look for the pieces in a garbage bag stashed in a juniper shrub outside. Just get me unstuck so I can get that ruby!" He was shaking with fury.

Ophelia was thrilled that Pierre had spilled the location of the Scarlet Claw pieces. It was all coming together! With the *Odds & Ends* box in her paws and intel on where the other two pieces were, the mission was done! And when she delivered everything to FFBI HQ, she'd be legendary!

But she hesitated before leaving the elevator shaft. The temptation to tease Pierre was too much.

WHOOSH. Still in the shadows, she slid open the top panel of the elevator and peered down at Pierre. Again, she made P.U.G. talk in Norman's voice.

"Follow me, P.U.G." Ophelia gracefully leaped out of the elevator and made her way to the library's main floor. *It's purr-fect. Pierre is stuck in the elevator. Those silly dogs are up in the attic looking for a box they won't find. And I'm about to make a quiet, stealthy exit.*

"Oscar," she updated her inventor via her mic. "We're on the stairs. Almost outside. We'll grab the Scarlet Claw pieces from the juniper bush and run to get our plane! You'll get a chuckle out of this. . . . I just told my first knock-knock joke!"

But as soon as the words *knock-knock* came out of her mouth, Ophelia's plan for a stealth exit went up in smoke, because, on the library's stairs, P.U.G. burst out into an old song: "What's New Pussycat?" With its (surprisingly robust) dance moves and huge voice, an audience quickly gathered to listen. Some people even started to dance.

In shock, Ophelia's eyes bulged out as big as her inventor's eyes. "What is *THIS*?!"

Oscar was impressed. "Go, disco king! Yay! It sounds exactly like Tomcat Jones."

"*Why on earth* is this metal horror show singing *TOMCAT JONES* while we are trying to make a stealthy escape?"

"Well, it took some brilliant coding," he bragged, "but dare I say, it was *you* who asked it to perform."

"What do you mean?" Ophelia asked, her voice shaking with fur-y.

"You must have inadvertently used the secret phrase," Oscar said, "which is ironic. I chose it because when I put it through my word algorithm, the results said the chance that you'd ever use it was miniscule."

"What's the code that makes P.U.G. sing?! What is the phrase?" Ophelia demanded.

"It's *knock-knock*. But P.U.G. would have had to hear it *three times*." Oscar bit his cheek to avoid laughing. "You *HATE* knock-knock jokes. The odds were high that you'd *never* say that phrase three times."

"Make this auditory abomination stop, fish." They tried to weave through the crowd. "We've got to get outside, get the Scarlet Claw pieces from the juniper bush, and get back to the jet. MEW is expecting us at FFBI HQ."

Without too much fuss, Oscar stopped P.U.G.'s impromptu concert, and the trio emerged outside to descend the library's front steps. But before they could get to the bottom, they were surrounded by dogs.

The CCIA had them cornered.

"Don't bother 'overcoming' your obstacles.
Stomp them into fine dust, add glitz,
and use as party confetti."

—Ophelia von Hairball V

16

RUFF & TUMBLE

Hello there, neighbor." Thug stepped forward through a wall of dogs to confront Ophelia. His smile was slow and his stance confident. "What are *you* doing here, at the New York Public Library?"

"Getting books like everyone else." Ophelia grinned. "Besides eating bonbons and abiding by the law, reading is my favorite hobby. And what a coincidence that *you're* here, too. You look a bit ruff, though. Like a square pug in a round hole. I thought you were busy playing poker with your buddies?"

Thug didn't miss a beat. The circle of CCIA agents continued to move in, tighter and tighter, on Ophelia, Oscar, and P.U.G. With the stress of being surrounded, Oscar crumpled to the ground and closed his eyes, but Ophelia remained cool.

"My buddies and I thought we'd come visit the big city and check out a few books, too. But if you don't mind, I'd like to take a look inside that box you're carrying. We have reason to believe you've got your paws on something that's not yours."

"Is that so?" Ophelia asked.

"The CCIA has been multiplying efforts to catch you in the act, Ophelia von Hairball V. I keep hearing you're the *number-one cat burglar in the world* and that *there's no stopping you*. But guess what? *Paw and order* will prevail. You can't keep breaking the rules! And this time we've caught you *red*-pawed, with a red ruby that doesn't belong to you."

Ophelia raised her perfectly manicured eyebrows. "I'm afraid you are confused. My colleague and I were just searching the library for information. You should find yourself better intel."

Thug's eyes popped out, but his voice remained calm. "I play poker. I know all about bluffing. Hand over the box."

Ophelia shrugged and removed the box from her bag, holding it out for Thug to take. "Here you go." Thug took the box from Ophelia's manicured claws. She looked at Oscar. "My fish-faced associate is very tired. If you don't mind, we'll be on our way. Perhaps we can catch up at home sometime?"

Thug smiled. "Oh, please don't go anywhere just yet. Because as soon as I prove you've got the ruby, I'm taking you into custody."

A flustered Pierre and seething Norman ran through the library doors and down the front steps.

Thug continued his threats. "Mark my words, Ophelia. Cat by cat, the CCIA will dismantle the FFBI. I'm happy to lead the charge."

Pierre piped up, "When that dismantling happens, *cousin*, it will take me no time at all to let the world know you've been bumped off your fancy-shmancy, number-one cat burglar pedestal!"

From the corner of her eye, Ophelia could see Oscar's S.P.I.T. full of frantic bubbles—a sure sign that he was stressed. "But you're a cat, too, Pierre," the fish piped up. "You're also an FFBI member."

Pierre snorted and stepped forward, toward Thug and the other CCIA dogs. His unibrow looked more menacing than ever. "Listen to me, dogs. I have a proposal."

Several sets of canine ears perked up. "As you know, Norman and I have the first two pieces of the Scarlet Claw." He rubbed his paws together. "It seems that you have the third piece. If we were to join forces, we'd have all three pieces. Right here, right now, on the steps of this library, we could put the Scarlet Claw together, make this laser pointer work, and gain control of *all cats*."

"If someone says you can't do something, do it twice. And wear a new outfit the second time."

—Ophelia von Hairball V

17

UN-FUR-TUNATE ALLIES

Ophelia couldn't help but groan. The fact that her ne-fur-ious cousin had offered to join the CCIA was one of the most preposterous notions she'd ever heard. He was a total disgrace to the FFBI.

The dogs had convened to the side of the steps to have a little secret discussion of Pierre's proposal.

Oscar propped himself up and leaned on P.U.G. "This is too much," Oscar lamented. "You were right about me traveling. I don't have the bubble-gumption to make it out in the field."

"Nonsense," Ophelia said. She winked at him. "You've got all the bubble-gumption in the world. Plus the outfits you design are stellar."

"Ophelia! Shouldn't we alert MEW and tell her what's happening? Your cousin is about to join the enemy! They're going to take over the world and destroy the FFBI and its legacy, not to mention they'll demolish your reputation!"

"Don't get all dramatic on me now, Oscar. They'll do nothing of the sort," Ophelia said, smoothing her eyelashes.

Suddenly the dogs broke up, and Thug stepped forward and shook Pierre's paw. "We agree that we can accomplish more if we work together," said Thug. "Temporarily, of course. Give us the base and the magnifier and we'll take down the FFBI."

Pierre beamed. Oscar shook his head. "Cat! If you give them the pieces, the CCIA will be able to control you, too!"

"Oh no, they won't," Norman retorted. The frog inventor ran to the juniper bush down the block, where they'd stashed the Scarlet Claw pieces. When he came back, he handed Pierre the two artifacts, then produced a pair of massive sunglasses. "Here," he said to Pierre. "These will block the ruby rays coming from the giant laser pointer. Wear them and you won't be affected by the Scarlet Claw."

He glared at Ophelia with big frog eyes. "*You*, on the other hand," he said smugly, "will be *fully* affected. And so will all the *other* cats in the FFBI." He turned to Oscar and boasted, "I was able to calculate the exact frequency that the ruby rays will emit. It was simple to create a countermeasure in the form of a special lens." He looked at Oscar and flicked his tongue. Oscar shook his head in disbelief.

"Once we put the Scarlet Claw together, you'll be utterly mesmerized," he explained.

"Norman!" Oscar threw his fins into the air and rolled his eyes to the sky. "You're an official FFBI inventor! You're sworn to uphold the mandate to help perform purr-fect crimes!"

Norman blinked a few long blinks and let out a defiant, evil ribbit. "Does that apply to *rejected* inventors? Some of us wouldn't mind a bit of revenge."

"Norman!" Pierre snapped his claws. "Hop to it! Time to work! Let's put this thing together and get on with world domination!"

Oscar raised his head and slowly got up. He stood in front of his cat burglar, never more serious. "Ophelia, if this is the last moment we have together as the dream team, I think I should be wearing my masterpiece in your honor." He pulled out an Oscar-size cat burglar suit that matched Ophelia's.

"Ta-da," he said, without his usual enthusiasm. She watched (with a teensy bit of horror) as he stepped into it and put a fin over his heart. "I want you to know, Ophelia von Hairball V of Burglaria: As your dedicated senior inventor, while you're under the spell of the Scarlet Claw, I'll tirelessly work to free you and all the other

cats from its enchantment." Then he crumpled once again. Ophelia rolled her eyes. The dogs turned their attention toward the box and broke the tape sealing it.

"Prepare for your doom, cousin!" Pierre stuck his tongue out at her. Norman ran to the box, his eyes popping out. But when the lid came off the box, *nobody* expected the prize that was inside.

"Darling, we cats need nine lives.
How else will we have time for all
the fun things we were born to do?"

—Ophelia von Hairball V

18

JUST KITTEN

"AAAAAAH! RUN FOR YOUR LIIIIIIIIVES!" Norman screamed, startled by the flapping of moth wings. Norman hopped up and down so hard that he dismantled the Scarlet Claw's base and magnifier, which flew into the air and landed hard at the bottom of the library's steps. One of the moths landed on his head, and Norman panicked. He did a spectacular flip-twirl combo before he hopped down the steps and jumped out of sight.

Pierre started to chase after him but stopped after a few feet and turned around. "Ophelia!" His hair was standing straight up and his back was arched in a menacing pose. Clutching Captain Claw-some in one paw, he shook the action figure

at her. "*You!* Always you! I will get you for this, Ophelia. I'll find a way to get revenge. Next time!"

Confused, Thug turned the *Odds & Ends* box upside down and shook it. Other than some moths, there was nothing in it.

Ophelia rolled her eyes. "Ruby? Oh, my dear dog. If you would have asked nicely, I could have told you about this box," she explained. "I donated several rare and valuable books to this library a few years ago but left the box here. But it's a purr-fect hat box, so I thought I'd come back and get it. Were you *really* expecting there to be a giant ruby inside an old, dusty, cardboard box in the attic of the New York Public Library?" She looked at the disappointed faces of the dogs that surrounded her.

"Awww," Ophelia responded with more than an ounce of sarcasm. "Look at those sad puppy-dog eyes! No wonder some find you doggone, irre-sistibly cute. Me? I'm immune." She nudged Oscar and stood tall. "Now. If you'll excuse us, please. My fish-ssistant has planned a vacation, and if we don't leave right now, we're going to miss our plane."

Without any evidence of wrongdoing, Thug and the CCIA agents couldn't detain Ophelia and her crew.

Ophelia, Oscar, and P.U.G. waltzed down the steps. If the dogs would have paid more attention, they'd have seen Oscar scoop up the two Scarlet Claw pieces before the trio disappeared down the busy sidewalk.

The gold was just starting to return to Oscar's face when they boarded their plane.

He checked the time. "What are we going to do? We have just enough time to get to Brussels. But we have only two pieces of the Scarlet Claw. Should we cancel?"

"Cancel?" Ophelia exclaimed, shocked. "Of course not. It's bad manners to cancel such an important appointment with so little notice. MEW is counting on us." She looked at the time, too. "But we'd better hurry."

"The true measure of success is in how you can make someone else shine on a bad day. That and the number of top burglar statues you own."

—Ophelia von Hairball V

19

CAT'S ALL, FOLKS

At FFBI HQ, MEW, Ophelia, Oscar, and P.U.G. were seated in MEW's opulent office. On her desk were the three pieces of the Scarlet Claw.

"The FFBI is grateful for your efforts, Ophelia. This was so much more than a regular heist."

"I'm happy I could help," said Ophelia. Oscar cleared his throat, and Ophelia smiled. "I mean,

we're happy we could help. Since the ruby doesn't actually belong to anyone, do you think, Director MEW, that there is any possible way I could keep it at my lair? It makes such a comfortable seat. And it matches my new rug." She glanced at Oscar. "You might remember that I lost my old one when a colleague made me use it as a parachute."

MEW hesitated. She pointed at a small symbol etched into the jewel. "See this? You know this is an ancient FFBI mark."

Ophelia nodded, intrigued. The FFBI Director

continued, "There are rumors of more treasures etched with this mark—all related to the lost city of Catlantis. But that legend is for a different day. Dare I ask how this ruby came to be in your possession?"

"Several years ago," Ophelia explained, "on another heist, I came across the box in the library. When Isaac mentioned the box called *Odds and Ends*, I almost fell over," she admitted. "I've had the ruby in my lair for some time."

MEW looked between Ophelia and Oscar. "I'd like you to keep it," she told her top cat burglar. "It matches your décor, and perhaps hiding it in plain sight isn't the worst idea after all. You *did* keep it safe. Also, if you feel like you can make your lair *very secure*, then you can keep your address, too—and stay living beside that CCIA dog. Who knows? We might be able to learn a few things about the way those dogs work."

Oscar leaned in and whispered, "I'll upgrade your security if you take me with you on your next heist."

Ophelia hesitated, then finally nodded.

"Director MEW, what will you do with the other pieces of the Scarlet Claw?" Ophelia inquired. "The CCIA is very interested in getting them."

"That's classified information," said MEW. "But don't fret. Until we figure out how our vault was compromised in the first place, we have taken extra measures to keep them safe." She looked at Ophelia, Oscar, and P.U.G. "You three better get home. There's quite a big competition coming up."

EPILOGUE

FFBI CAT BURGLAR TIP: There is nothing better than a good catnap, a great manicure, and knowing that, no matter what, you're always a powerful force in the world.

LOOK FOR THE NEXT MISSION!

Ophelia von Hairball V of Burglaria

— in —

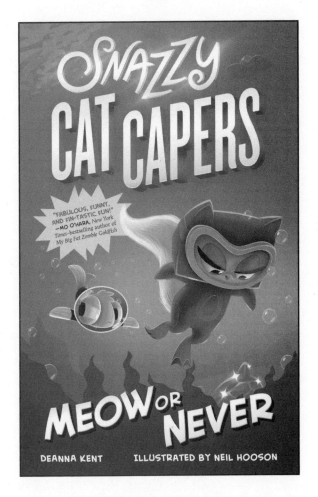

COMING IN 2020!

ACKNOWLEDGMENTS

Super-sparkle thanks to Gemma Cooper of the Bent Agency and to Macmillan's Imprint team—especially Erin Stein, Nicole Otto, and Natalie C. Sousa. Working with you all is a dream.

#teamworkmakesthedreamwork

ABOUT THE AUTHOR & ILLUSTRATOR

DEANNA KENT and **NEIL HOOSON** have worked on books, brand and marketing campaigns, and interactive experiences. Deanna loves twinkle string lights, black licorice, and Edna Mode, and she may be the only person on the planet who says "teamwork makes the dream work" without a hint of sarcasm. Neil is king of a Les Paul guitar, makes killer enchiladas, and really wants aliens to land in his backyard. By far, their greatest creative challenge is raising four (very busy, very amazing) boys. Snazzy Cat Capers is their first chapter book series.

BFFFFs

OSCAR FISHGERALD GOLD

INVENTOR ACADEMY GRAD
WITH THE SECOND-HIGHEST MARK EVER

2ND PLACE
INVENTOR ACADEMY

REMINDER
SCHEDULED P.U.G.
MAINTENANCE